D0284918

Tinker Bell

STARRING

Vidia

Iridessa

Rosetta

Queen Clarion

First published by Parragon in 2009
Parragon, Queen Street House, 4 Queen Street, Bath BA1 1HE, UK

Copyright © 2009 Disney Enterprises, Inc.
From Walt Disney's masterpiece "Peter Pan".
Visit www.DisneyFairies.com

All rights reserved. No part of this publication may be reproduced, stored in a retrieval system or transmitted, in any form or by any means, electronic, mechanical, photocopying, recording or otherwise, without the prior permission of the copyright holder.

ISBN 978-1-4075-3228-8

Printed in China

Disney
fairies

TinkerBell

Adapted by
Lisa Marsoli

Illustrated by
The Disney Storybook Artists

Bath · New York · Singapore · Hong Kong · Cologne · Delhi · Melbourne

One winter's day in London, a baby laughed for the very first time. That laugh floated up and away to meet its destiny. It would become a fairy, just like all first laughs.

It flew straight for the Second Star to the Right, and passed through it in a burst of light. On the other side was . . . Never Land!

The laugh floated towards a magical place in the heart of the island. This was Pixie Hollow, home of the fairies!

Vidia, the fastest flying fairy of them all, guided the arrival into the Pixie Dust Tree. There, a dust-keeper named Terence sprinkled it with pixie dust, and it took the shape of a tiny, adorable fairy.

Clarion, queen of the fairies, helped the newcomer unfurl her two gossamer wings. The new fairy flapped her wings and realized she could fly!

Queen Clarion waved her hand, and several toadstools sprung up around the Pixie Dust Well. Fairies immediately fluttered forwards to place different objects on the pedestals. Rosetta, a garden fairy, brought a flower. Silvermist, a water fairy, carried a droplet of water. Iridessa, a light fairy, placed a lamp on her pedestal.

"They will help you find your talent," the queen explained to the new fairy.

The youngster timidly placed her hand on a beautiful flower. Its glow instantly faded. She reached for a water droplet, but that, too, faded.

The fairy moved on without touching anything else – she was afraid to fail again – but then something amazing happened. As she passed by a hammer, it began to glow. Then it rose up off its pedestal and flew straight for her!

"I've never seen one glow that much before," said Silvermist.

"I do believe you're right," agreed Rosetta. "Li'l daisy-top might be a very rare talent indeed!"

Vidia glowered. She had one of the strongest and rarest talents in Pixie Hollow, and she wasn't looking for competition.

"Tinker fairies," called the queen. "Welcome the newest member of your talent guild – Tinker Bell!"

A large fairy named Clank and a bespectacled fairy named Bobble came forwards to greet Tink. Then they whisked her off for a flying tour of Pixie Hollow. It was almost time for the changing of the seasons, and they could see everyone getting ready.

Finally, the trio landed at Tinkers' Nook. Tink looked around and saw fairies fixing and fashioning all kinds of amazing, useful objects.

Next Clank and Bobble took Tinker Bell to her own little house, which had a closet filled with clothes. The garments turned out to be much too big, but Tink knew just how to fix them.

Tinker Bell put on her new dress and tied her hair up. Then she reported to the workshop. Clank and Bobble couldn't wait to show her all the handy things that tinker fairies made.

Soon Fairy Mary – the no-nonsense fairy who ran Tinkers' Nook – arrived. She noticed the new fairy's dainty hands. "Don't worry, dear, we'll build up those tinker muscles in no time," she exclaimed.

Then, after reminding Clank and Bobble to make their deliveries, she was gone.

A little while later, Tink, Clank and Bobble were on their way. Luckily they had Cheese the mouse – and Clank – to pull the loaded wagon.

PITTER-PATTER! PITTER-PATTER!

The friends heard a sound behind them.

"Sprinting Thistles! **Aaaaagh**!" screamed Clank. The weeds nearby had come to life and were headed straight for them! The wagon pitched this way and that. Then it lurched down the path and landed in a flowerbed in Springtime Square.

Rosetta, Silvermist, Iridessa and Fawn rushed over to help their friends. The tinkers were unhurt, and soon ready to go back to their deliveries. There were rainbow tubes for Iridessa, milkweed-pod satchels for Fawn and pussy-willow brushes for Rosetta.

Iridessa explained that she would roll up rainbows, put them in the tubes, and take them to the mainland.

"What's the mainland?" Tink asked.

"It's where we're going to go for spring, to change the seasons," replied Silvermist.

Next the tinkers stopped at the Flower Meadow, where Vidia was vacuuming the pollen out of flowers with her whirlwind.

Tinker Bell startled Vidia, and the just-filled pots fell over.

"Hi! What's your talent?" Tink asked.

"I am a fast-flying fairy. Fairies of every talent depend on me," answered Vidia. She made it clear that she didn't think much of tinker fairies.

Tink was insulted. "When I go to the mainland, I'll prove just how important we are!" she replied.

Tink flew off, grumbling to herself. Soon, however, something down on the beach caught her attention. When she landed, she discovered several wonderful treasures buried in the sand.

"Lost Things," said Clank when Tink brought her finds to the Tinkers' Nook workshop. "They wash up on Never Land from time to time," explained Bobble.

Fairy Mary whisked the trinkets away. The queen's review of the springtime preparations was that night, and there was a lot to do.

Tink decided this was her chance to prove to Vidia just how important a tinker's talent really was!

That evening, the Minister of Spring welcomed Queen Clarion to the review ceremony.

"I think you'll find we have things well in hand," he said proudly. "When the Everblossom blooms, we will be ready to bring spring to the mainland."

Suddenly, Tinker Bell interrupted the proceedings. "I came up with some fantastic things for tinkers to use when we go to the mainland!" she told the queen excitedly.

Tink pulled a homemade paint sprayer out of the wagon and demonstrated it on a flower that needed coloring. But instead of spraying paint, it exploded.

"Has no one explained?" Queen Clarion said gently. "Tinker fairies don't go to the mainland. All of those things are done by the nature-talent fairies. I'm sorry."

The next morning, Tink asked her friends to teach her how to be a nature fairy. She really wanted to go to the mainland. Reluctantly, the other fairies agreed to help. No fairy had ever changed his or her talent before!

Tink's first lesson was on how to become a water fairy. Silvermist showed her how to place a dewdrop on a spider's web, but each time Tink tried, the dewdrop burst.

The light-fairy lesson didn't go any better. Tink lost control of the light and attracted a group of fireflies. They thought Tink's glow was irresistible!

Fawn had Tink's animal fairy lesson all planned. "We're teaching baby birds how to fly," she announced.

Fawn went to a nest, smiled at a bird, and gently encouraged it until the fluffy little creature was flying along right behind her.

Unfortunately, Tink's baby bird seemed terrified. When she nudged it towards the edge of the nest, it even tried to fight her!

"If I end up making acorn kettles the rest of my life, I am holding you personally responsible," Tinker Bell said impatiently.

Tink looked up and saw a majestic bird soaring in the sky. She decided she would ask it to help her teach the baby bird.

Suddenly an ear-splitting screech filled the forest. The bird was a hawk!

Tink hurtled down into the knothole of a tree – but Vidia was already hiding there. Soon the hawk discovered them both, so they jumped down a tunnel inside the tree. When Vidia reached the end of the chute, she could see the hawk outside. She stopped in the nick of time – but Tink accidentally slammed into her and sent Vidia shooting out of the tree. The hawk opened its beak, ready to strike. Luckily, the other fairies were able to chase the bird off.

A little while later, Tinker Bell sat on the beach. "Great," she muttered. "At this rate, I should get to the mainland right about, oh, never!"

She angrily threw a pebble and heard a **CLUNK**! Tink went to investigate and found a broken porcelain box.

By the time her friends found her, Tinker Bell was busily putting her discovery back together. The final touch was a lovely porcelain ballerina that fit into the lid. Tinker Bell gave the dancer a spin, and to her delight, the box played music!

"Do you even realize what you're doing?" asked Rosetta. "Fixing stuff like this – that's what tinkering is!"

"Who cares about going to the mainland anyway?" Silvermist added.

Tink realized her friends didn't want her to change talents. Desperate, she went to visit the only fairy she thought might be able to help.

But Vidia was not in the mood for visitors – especially Tinker Bell.

"You're my last hope," pleaded Tink. "Rosetta won't even try to teach me to be a garden fairy now."

That gave Vidia an idea. She suggested that Tinker Bell prove she was a garden fairy by capturing the Sprinting Thistles.

Tink knew this was her last chance to get to go to the mainland. She built a corral and made a lasso. She rode Cheese into Needlepoint Meadow and used twigs to herd a pair of Thistles into the corral.

"It's working!" Tink cried joyfully. But as she headed back out into the meadow, Vidia quietly blew open the corral gate. The two Thistles ran right out.

Soon other Thistles joined the two that had escaped. It was a stampede!

"Wait! Come back!" yelled Tinker Bell, riding after them.

The Thistles headed to Springtime Square, where they trampled over the carefully organized springtime supplies.

Just then, Queen Clarion appeared. A look of shock crossed her face. "By the Second Star . . . all the preparations for spring –!"

"I'm sorry," Tink whispered as she took to the sky.

Tink decided to leave Pixie Hollow forever, but she couldn't go without one last visit to the workshop. She had to admit that she did love to tinker.

At the workshop, she noticed Cheese sniffing around something at the back of the room – it was trinkets Fairy Mary had taken from her on her first day in Pixie Hollow.

"Lost Things . . . that's it!" she cried as she took them over to her worktable. Tink thought she had an idea that would fix everything.

That night, Queen Clarion gathered all the fairies and explained that spring would not come that year. There simply wasn't enough time to replace all the supplies that had been ruined.

"**Wait!**" Tinker Bell cried. "I know how we can fix everything!" The clever fairy had designed speedy machines to fix what the Thistles had trampled. She had even used Lost Things to repair her paint sprayer.

Vidia was furious. "Corral the Thistles . . ." she muttered, "I should have told you to go after the hawk!"

Queen Clarion heard this, and looked sharply at Vidia. "I think your fast-flying talent is well-suited to chasing down each and every one of the Thistles," she said sternly.

Tink showed a group of fairies how to assemble a machine to make berry paint. Next she rigged up a vacuum that could collect huge amounts of seeds at a time.

The fairies worked all night using Tink's machines. Early the next morning, Queen Clarion and the ministers of the seasons flew into the square. Before them were more springtime supplies than they had ever seen!

The sun rose, and the Everblossom opened and gave off a golden glow, signaling that it was time to bring springtime to the world.

The fairies cheered.

"You did it, Tinker Bell," congratulated Queen Clarion.

"We all did it," Tink replied.

"Queen Clarion," said Silvermist. "Can't Tink come with us to the mainland?"

"It's okay," Tink protested. "My work is here."

Fairy Mary flew over, looking sternly at Tink. "I don't think so, missy!" she said. She gave a little whistle, and Clank and Bobble led in the wagon. Tink's music box was inside, all polished and shiny.

"I'd imagine there's someone out there who's missing this. Perhaps a certain tinker fairy has a job to do after all . . . on the mainland," said Fairy Mary.

The nature fairies and Tink went to London. They spread out over the city to deliver their springtime magic.

Tinker Bell found the home where the music box belonged, and tapped on the windowpane. A little girl named Wendy Darling poked her head out of the window. Tink watched from her hiding place as Wendy's face filled with happiness at the discovery of her long-lost treasure. The girl took a small key from a chain around her neck and turned it in a slot. The music box began to play!

Soon the fairies' work was done and it was time for them all to return to Never Land. Tink couldn't wait to get home – she had lots of tinkering to do!